The Red Thread

Robert MacDonald

Copyright © 2016 Robert MacDonald

All rights reserved.

ISBN-13: 978-1533448163
ISBN-10: 1533448167

DEDICATION

For Family And Friends

THE RED THREAD

CONTENTS

Prologue

The Support Group

The Care Facility

Orvar

Bell Bottoms And Dancing

On A Mission

Something Moves Across The Floor

Ding, Ding, Ding

She Makes It Easy For Him

ACKNOWLEDGMENTS

I wish to personally thank the following people for their contributions to my inspiration and knowledge, and others' help in creating this book: Mary Kenny, Phil, Darrell, Carolina, Robbie, Carol, Rosemary, Wendy, Allithia, Dorothy, Mike, Makiko, Ken and Nina.

Cover photo by Phil Kenny

Special Thanks to Marion Quednau

PROLOGUE

Tuesday after supper he drives his car to the church, and idles, undecided. There are no lights on in the main sanctuary. He's relieved. He can get the hell out of there. Then he sees a light at the side door. Someone peeking a head out as if they're expecting him.

Damn, he thinks.

A small woman—she's got to be in her seventies, but still trim, buttoned up tight in a pant suit—is marshalling chairs in a circle. The place has a damp, musty carpet smell of religion about it. He used to believe. It's up in the air now. His faith in anything.

"Dr. West send you? Welcome," she says. "I'm Helen McKinnon." Then she points to a man sitting limply, eyes downcast. No expression. "My husband, Jim."

The man smiles bleakly, his hand shaking to beat the band as he offers it in greeting.

Just looking at this fellow is like looking at his future. He wants to turn on his heel and leave.

Helen picks up a marker pen and name tag that begins, "Hello, I'm …."

"Name's Lewis. Lewis with an "e."" He changed it from the small-town spelling, and his father's name, "Louis," years ago. Didn't want to be a chip off the old block.

Helen is making a big fuss setting up. Upsets the donation can; a few coins hit the floor, roll away.

"Sorry about that," she says crisply. She's got that Brit accent, and is picking up the spilled change. She's obviously doing this whole shtick for her husband. Devoted.

Others are drifting in – and drifting's a good word

for it. They're shuffling, unsteady on their feet, and their voices are quiet mutters, another Parkinson's trait. And there's staring. A lot of staring. Checking out who's worse. Or who's not so bad. Yet.

Helen doesn't waste any time. She knows it's in short supply.

"The topic tonight is "Advances in Research." She indicates a pile of pamphlets on the table.

Sounds promising, Lewis thinks, bleakly. He's trying to be positive, but it's a hard fit. He stands, his eyes intent on the door. It's now or never. And the meeting hasn't even begun.

"Oh yes," Helen says, not missing a beat. "Let me introduce our newcomer tonight, Lewis ..."

"Lewis with an "e," her husband adds, with a raspy laugh.

"Tell us something about yourself, Lewis with an "e," she says.

He's caught now. "I'm tired. Wake up tired – can't focus. My legs are tired. Weak. But I guess you can all relate to this."

Everyone nods. And for some reason he feels angry with the whole lot of them. The "circle of bobbing heads."

A fellow named Jeff, his head jerking mightily and body twitches galore, asks brightly, "Have you been to the university research centre?"

"No, I go next week," says Lewis, his voice seeming overly-loud, as if he's shouting.. "How 'bout you? Have you been there?"

"I went last year," Jeff says, his voice a near-whisper. "They've been a great help."

A pasty-faced woman with too much make-up

starts to sniffle, as if something is caught in her throat. She's sitting off-kilter in her chair, as if she's in a strong wind. "Oh, I've done my research," she blurts out. Full-out sobbing now. Her thin chest heaving.

"He's met someone. My husband. I can just tell. I don't know what I'm going to do."

Helen moves to hug her, briskly, efficiently. It's probably in her instruction manual.

Lewis knocks into his chair, clumsily, as he heads for the door with that slap-footed gait of his. There are whispers behind him, but he's not looking back. Screw them.

Helen follows him to the door, pulls at his sleeve.

"I'm too young for this crap," Lewis says. "I just want my life back."

"We all want our lives back, " she says, as the door shudders behind him.

Three nights' dishes in the sink, crumbs from last night's peanut butter sandwich on the counter. Piles of handwritten notes, journals, a mountain of paper clutter on the table. There's barely room for his coffee mug. He slips on his navy cardigan, wool-lined slippers. There's a chill in the air.

Lucky Lou knows his routine by heart – there's a deep sigh of satisfaction from under the covers as he heads out the door. *There he goes, but he'll be back—* .

The long corridor to the lounge is silent at this time of the morning, so he can hear his own slow progress, an off-beat drop-foot that slaps the floor. Ka-shunk, ka-shunk .

The night shift worker sometimes nods off for a bit, then makes the first pot of coffee at 5 AM. It's a cat-and-mouse game they play, to see if the care aide's awake or if Lewis slept in. He can tell by the way the creamers and cups are laid out, who's on that night. But this morning it's mystery – the dishes look like the tail-end of a lively picnic.

There's a shape in the recliner all right, wrapped in a blanket. But the form has braids – Lewis is startled to see her there. It's Nicole. His favourite. Usually on day-shift. She must have been called in to cover for someone.

She senses his presence, rears up in her chair.

"Geez!" she sputters, embarrassed. "You scared me. What's wrong? Is anything wrong?"

Lewis motions with his hand. "Sorry, stay put. I'll put the coffee on."

It's against the rules, but Lewis has earned certain privileges. Nicole mumbles "okay," and rolls over, trying to catch a few more minutes of sleep. She's probably exhausted from one of her crazy cycling trips. How she finds the energy, after leaving this whole rigmarole of giving pills and making beds, to pedal anywhere, beats him. But he likes to think of her in high gear, always game to take something on. It doesn't hurt to think.

He once asked her about the braids, thought she was Swedish.

"Wrong kind of braids," she'd said, laughing. "I'm half Cherokee."

Her eyes had confused him. Crystal blue. Always looking straight through him, or that's how it seemed.

He'd felt totally stupid, but she didn't hold it against him.

Nicole is restrained, almost verging on shy, in her day-to-day duties, compared with some of the others, more bossy or take-charge. But she isn't an innocent, either, he figures. Has some life story to her. Fact is, she has kids. And no father in sight, as far as he knows.

But he keeps his interest in Nicole to himself. It's hard to maintain any kind of privacy in this place. A small community of 160 suites where he's a "resident." Everybody older than him by a stretch, everybody into everyone else's business.

He takes a few sips before heading back. He'd like to bring Nicole a cup; it would seem intimate somehow. But he watches her face at rest, with those lovely high cheekbones. No, he'll let her sleep.

He has the top corner suite on the third floor. No one on three sides, and with that extra window, feeling larger than the others. He calls it The Penthouse.

His Jack Russell bounces off the bed at his return. She stretches with that screeching yawn she has, expecting to be fed. She's so smart she probably knows it's Sunday: the aroma of sizzling bacon soon. The cook always saving a strip or two for Lucky.

Lewis stares out the window to the darkness. The cook will be in early to help unload the food order. Twice a week, a semi arrives at the back of the building, the silence broken by the huff and puff of air brakes. It's a tricky angle to negotiate, and new drivers often hit the building. That's the only bit of excitement around the place.

Everyday it's the same. Like a scene from the movie, *Ground Hog Day*, without the funny parts. He has a small dog for company and is grateful for it, which feels pathetic somehow. As sad as the way the place looks, a real shambles with all the newspapers and manuscripts spread out on every surface, even the floor.

He wants to finish his novel, thinks maybe he can find a signal or sign in the writing that will free him up again. All his life he's been a real go-getter, relying on his wits. Determined. The "comeback kid." Failing high school English, then writing for a newspaper. Building a magazine business from scratch against the odds. A specialty mag – holistic health. It seems sadly ironic now.

He turns from the dark glass of the window and sees himself in the mirror. Heavier. Friar Tuck-like. Unshaven. Holding a slim book given to him by an old lady at church. Years ago. Some nineteenth century evangelist dissecting the notion of love. Still unread. Lewis has only picked it up again because the poor fellow died young.

Jesus, something has to give. He'll do it, one shelf at a time. Clean up this clutter. Finish something and start something new. *He will become his own door, he thinks.*

Now that's a good line—poetic. He should put it in his novel, build on it.

His mind wanders, and he thinks again of Nicole, probably up and bustling by now. It doesn't hurt to think.

The phone rings. He tries to ignore it. Once, twice, won't stop.

"Hello, Orvar."

The turkey calls him as he leaves his garage in his luxury SUV with his hands-free phone. At 7:25 every day, like clockwork. He pretends it's concern, but it's really just meddling.

"Are you finished yet?" Orvar's tone is condescending. He's a prairie redneck, transplanted to the west coast. Thinks Lewis has become too *airy-fairy*. Razzes him about his writing. Doesn't have a clue.

"Still working on it. I have enough for three books. It helps the chatter in my mind –helps organize my thoughts. Which reminds me – How's Eva and the kids?"

Orvar, married, house in the burbs, goldfish in the bowl for the brats, healthy cash flow. And *he's* healthy. Big bonus. He's a man of substance. But unhappy.

Always ranting about his marriage. Some little tit-for-tat.

"Still working on it," Orvar says, cut short. Sounding wounded.

There's a click on the line. Silence.

Serves him right, Lewis thinks. He's not supposed to call in the morning, when I'm scribbling. But does anyway. Just to bug me. He's so frigging stubborn.

They've been friends for close to fifty years. Since the third grade, when they spent almost every day together. Lewis always thinks of the time they built the snow fort. More of a burrowing into the big drifts, but never mind. It was something to do in a cold prairie winter. It took them the whole weekend, and they were proud of it.

Lewis, the smaller of two, was the decision-maker. The brains beside the brawn, he's always said, just to bother Orvar. It was Lewis that wanted to finish the tunnel. He was digging frantically while Orvar stood watch. What exactly he was watching for, Lewis can't quite remember. Maybe some bigger kids who used to bother them sometimes in their foolish games. Anyway, Orvar looked away for just a minute, at a snowplough that went by on the road. And when he looked back, the whole fort had collapsed on Lewis, burying him. It was a mountain of snow. And the only thing that saved the day was a dot of red, a strand from a hand-knitted mitten. It caught Orvar's eye. And he pulled a sputtering Lewis out to safety.

Although Orvar always says that's not how it went. They can never agree on what actually happened.

A gentle knock on the door. Lewis jumps at the sound. Feels guilty for reading his horoscope, when he's procrastinating on his daily grind of a few hundred words.

More times than not, the fellow who writes for the local paper, has had an inkling. Not exactly bang-on, but still. Close enough to give him goose-bumps. Today his oracle says: "Be careful, you might fall. You need to be grounded. The whole world seems to be giving way. A Taurus will need your help."

Very funny, he thinks. I'm close to falling all the time, and I'm the one who needs help. He knows depression is one of the dead ends of the disease, and tries to shrug it off.

The sound of keys and the deadbolt releases.

"Don't turn that big light on," Lewis says, without looking up. "Or touch anything," he adds, as if it's a crime scene.

"Are we in a bad mood?"

It's a familiar voice, blunt, with a bit of mischief thrown into the mix.

He turns quickly, smiles sheepishly, to see it's Nicole. She's fidgeting with her charts. Pinning the hair that's strayed out of her braids. She looks a little out-of-sorts herself.

"You still here? Wow! They sure got you working."

She slides open the kitchen drawer. Lays out his morning pills. "They mixed up the scheduling. So I've had to cover. It never rains, it pours." A long sigh, although she never complains.

Right out of the blue, he blurts out. "Hey, what's your sign? You know, astrology. All that stuff about the stars and the moon in the right place..."

"An exhausted Taurus," she says.

Lewis smiles. "Go figure. My horoscope said you'd be along." It might be in the cards, not just a fluke, the urge to give her coffee this morning.

"And you?"

"A grumpy Cancer," he says. "We're intuitive. Oversensitive. Sorry I groused at you."

"No problem," she says.

And the neat thing about Nicole is that she means it. There's only ten years' difference in their ages, he figures. Give or take. And who knows? The horoscope bunff might be a push in the right direction.

No doubt Nicole can feel the attention Lewis throws her way. It could make things uncomfortable, but she's a pro.

"Your meds are out on the counter, okay? Pretend I wasn't here, and you can get back to work."

It's growing light outside the windows, buds on the trees after six months of rain. And he doesn't really want to get back to work.

"Did I hear you have a show at the gallery?" Lewis asks. "This weekend?"

"I wish," Nicole says. "No, no. I just have one of my pieces on exhibit."

"I think you should have your own show," Lewis says. "Your work's unique, one-of-a-kind. I love the bit I've seen." He smiles encouragement at her.

"Blobs of mud and clay," she says, blushing at the compliment. She hurries out the door, leaving her keys in the drawer. Comes back a second later, smiling, saying, "Duh. Must be tired, I guess."

"No small wonder," Lewis says.

"Hey, I'd be willing to give you a hand, organizing – helping you put some stuff away. Laundry, anything that might be helpful. Tomorrow after three o'clock – if that works for you. I'm good at that sort of thing." She seems to be looking at his mess. Pointedly. The writing stuff strewn everywhere. "Still working on that book?"

"Don't ask," Lewis says.

Nicole stares a hole through Lewis. Gently closes her eyes then and says, "To thine own self be true. Most people don't get it – not even my family."

He's a bit startled to hear the word, *family.* Knew she had the two kids, wonders if she has a partner.

"My mother says my spare time belongs to the boys," Nicole says, as if she can read his mind. "I tell her I have more to give if I take a little puttering time for myself."

"You're right," Lewis says. "Pisses me off when people ask if I'm finished yet, as if I'm some widget factory."

"Screw 'em," she says. "By the way, what's your novel about?" She's hovering in the doorway, as if she has all the time in the world to hear the answer.

"It might sound weird," Lewis says. "But I'm writing about this...the *red thread*, as my father used to call it. The thing that pulls you through." And he shrugs, feels stupid even having admitted it.

She smiles. "You're an artist, Lewis. Writing the truth."

Lewis watches her walk down the hall with her perfect posture, as if she's balancing books on her head.

And this despite being up all night.

She's carrying all her charts in what he calls her "hippy-dippy bag," woven of bright colours, and hanging off one shoulder as though she's carrying goods in a foreign market. She's her own person all right, one of a kind.

It flatters his ego, but it bothers him too. That Nicole called him an artist. Because now he has to live up to it. And he's getting nowhere.

He's tried to write this scene a million times in his head and it won't come close to the real deal. All the tangled sensations of that night.

He heard singing as he did his flap-foot into the building, the music wartime songs, not from his era. The room decorated with hearts, red and white carnations in skinny vases with pink ribbons. Valentine's Day.

He'd have no interest in this nonsense except for Nicole showing up in something other than her care-worker uniform. He knew she had a real life beyond this place.

She was wearing bell-bottoms, a baby doll blouse, as if she'd just walked out of a flower-power rally. Only she could pull it off – not concerned about the style of the time, just being herself.

Lewis hadn't forgotten what it was like to be younger, hoping at a dance. He sat beside the antique buffet, coffee in hand, feeling as beige as the wall. He killed some time

shooting the breeze with Eddie, as Eddie would say. He was a spry ninety-something, still unbelievably dapper; Oxford-cloth shirts, sharp crease in his gray flannels. Intelligent, no lazy brain. And still nimble on his feet too, galloping along without a walker or anything, often down at the gym doing his limbering exercises.

"That damn food truck hit the building again,"

Eddie said, nodding toward an elegant woman half his age who kept floating by on the arm of one of the residents. "I had to drive a big rig in tighter spaces, with bombs falling all around," he added. Eddie was a procurement officer in the war, and no doubt got his goods delivered on target.

"It's the training route," Lewis said, tongue-in-cheek. "My suite is right above the loading dock. It rattled my bed when it hit the wall—I thought we were having a major quake," he added.

"Same guy as last week," Eddie said. "Something needs to be done."

Oh something needed to be done, all right. Lewis saw Nicole walking in his direction—not in her nursing shoes, but in cute tennis sneakers.

She leaned over him, taking a sip of water from her bottle, one of those deals you snap on a bike frame. "Wanna dance, cowboy?"

"I'd wear you out," Lewis said.

Nicole smirked, daring him to get up and join the slow parade fox-trotting around the place. Strut his stuff.

He used to ooze confidence on the notion of taking a woman in his arms and making all the right moves, but now his heart wasn't in it. He didn't want to trip her up with his clown-footed gait, be pitied. Act like a fool.

And dancing always reminded him, whether he liked it or not, of Gabriela. The "Spanish dove," as he used to call her. She was the one who taught him the salsa, working only the hips. They won competitions, they were hot, and in tune. Until they weren't —until she packed up and went back to El Salvador. It took him ages to sort himself out, he'd fallen so hard.

Nicole was still standing there, not taking no for an answer, swaying back and forth, shifting her body in invitation.

"I used to own the floor," he said to her, his voice thickening with regret. "And now I'm just renting,... I'll take a pass."

"No worries," Nicole said, taking the pressure off. "I'll catch you later."

Just at that moment, to cap things off, Eddie went flying by with that woman he'd been eyeing; they were light on their feet, laughing, having a swell time.

He'd like to rewrite the whole evening, lose his self-pity and sweep Nicole into his arms. But it would be cheating on the real gambit — and now that Nicole's called him on it, he has to write what's true.

Lucky stares at Lewis. He tries to ignore her, but she's locked on. He feels her penetrating eyes. Probably bored. He slams his pen down.

"What? Do you want out? Gotta go? What's the matter?"

Her tail speeds up, then a loud screeching bark. And slams her paws, like peg legs, into his body. Jumping up against him. Then sitting and whimpering, ears perked.

"You're acting psycho. Go lie down in your bed," Lewis says firmly, pointing to her little curl-up spot.

But she refuses. Still staring, tail pointed, alert.

The lights flicker.

"Oh no, not the power," Lewis mutters. "Damn! That's all I need. Blow my hard drive—lose my work." He feels like he's actually written a good paragraph or two, might be on a roll.

He smells something burning. Probably someone down the hall charring their toast. It happens all the time.

Lucky's revved up again, running back and forth, barking frantically.

"Settle down," Lewis warns. "Shhhh...You'll wake everybody up."

But she's nudging the door and pawing in mid-air, practically turning cartwheels.

Another whiff. Like rubber burning …. Electrical?

"The damned fire alarm is going to go off any minute," Lewis says, as if to remind himself for the umpteenth time that he wishes he didn't live in this rookery of old folks.

He hears the gismo in his door click; then the strobe light for the hard-of-hearing and the fire siren start up –it's unbearable.

A loud blast, like a bomb. Car alarms going off in the neighbourhood.

What the heck's going on? His swivel chair and desk start to jimmy across the floor; there's a tinkling noise like glasses tapping together at a wedding. His hanging lamp in the dining room sways.

Power flickers back on. Then completely out.

He has to get the hell out of here.

A picture and flower vase on top of the fridge smash to the floor. Glass everywhere. Lucky barking hysterically and running through the shards. As if she sees a ghost in the room.

A deep crackling sound outside that raises the hair on his arms. A wave moves through the building like a knife cutting a cake in two.

Lewis grabs his wallet and jacket. Snaps Lucky's leash on her harness. He's barely keeping his balance, like a sailor come back to dry land. And the land's moving.

But strangely he hasn't felt this light on his feet in ages. Adrenalin. They head out the door, the frame shaking like it's going to come down on them.

He's shouting, "Earthquake! Earthquake!" to no one in particular. And everyone.

No lights in the corridor; it's dusk-coloured. Eerie.

He heads past Dorothy's suite, Lucky straining at the leash by the door. It's where she gets a treat every morning. But there's no sign of Dot; she's completely deaf without her hearing aids.

He knows that and still he's banging on the door, shouting, "Dot, get up! We have to get out of here!"

Lucky's bouncing at the door handle, her high-pitched barking getting them nowhere. And then it happens. Lewis watches a huge crack open up in the wall; the hallway looks like an aluminum can that's slowly being twisted.

The only good part is Dot standing there, looking dazed behind the gaping hole.

"What's happening?"

"It's a quake, we've got to get out!" Lewis shouts into her ear.

Dot hasn't the faintest where her walker is, in all the dust, the crackling drywall still heaving. So he lets go Lucky's leash, helps Dot along, feeling his way along the handrails mounted on the heaving walls. Dot's small and frail; it feels as though she might slip away from him.

Lucky's gone screeching down the corridor, and Lewis is shouting at her to come back. Trying to stay level-headed. Pretending it's a walk in the woods, when the terrier goes ahead and then looks for approval, comes running back.

But he's lost sight of her, and he can hear screaming as he passes doors still closed, but strangely buckled.

He's yelling, "Get under a table! Brace yourselves! Earthquake!" But he feels helpless shouting into the gloom

And then a familiar voice, "Yes, yes. I'm coming. Get yourselves to the lounge; we're meeting in the lounge!" Nicole, rallying the residents to some sort of chaotic order.

"Lewis! You've got Dot, that's great. First everyone hitting their alarm buttons—and now with the power out, I can't tell who needs help!"

"Where's the frickin' staff? Where are the other nurses?" he protests. He can feel her panic, just below the surface.

"One of the girls says there's a raging fire in Complex Care; I guess they're all there!"

There's a group milling in front of the elevator, with their canes and walkers, but the elevator's shut off. In the lounge beyond he can see the pranged piano for singalongs, half on its side, wires sprung, the fake Chippendale chairs in a clutter in one corner, as if the floor might be tilting one way. The stoic picture of the Queen, with her crown and single strand of pearls, hanging off one hook and swinging eerily.

Nicole yells, "Lewis, get everybody together! We've got to move fast here!"

One lady—she doesn't cope well on the best of days, has dementia—is whimpering, "Do you know who I am? Do you know who I am?"

"Yes, I know you," Lewis offers, and he tries to take her by the hand, but she pulls away. God, how does Nicole do it? He's only had her job for five minutes and already he's feeling bushed.

He takes the woman more forcibly by the arm, but there's nowhere to sit her down, just a jumble of fallen furniture. He's relieved to see Lucky in the fray, someone petting her, just to keep themselves calm.

Nicole flings open the door to the stairwell, and the first woman she tries to help make her way down, stumbles and shrieks, nearly falls to the first landing. This is going to take forever, Lewis thinks, and they don't have forever.

He hears the sound of a chopper, moving fast. Looks out the window, the glass crazed. It's a yellow Coast Guard helicopter, another close behind. Lewis stares, and realizes the huge Douglas fir that everyone complained about, blocking the views of the ocean, is gone. Disappeared. Instead a mountain of newly moved earth. It's like looking at the lawn on its side.

Nicole's standing beside him, watching the choppers leave them behind. "I can't get half these people down the stairs," she says, her voice jerking. "They're too frail. And phones aren't working, all digital down …My boys," she adds. "I'm worried."

"That's probably where the choppers are going," Lewis says, inventing a little bravery, for her sake. "To the school—they'll be fine."

"You're right," Nicole says, her usual resolve clicking in again. "We have to worry about us. Find a way out."

The clock on the wall stopped at 7:54 AM. Just minutes before a shift change, so maybe some of the staff never even arrived. That's the not-so-great news for those stuck inside.

Even worse is the information from outside. Eddie's been on his ham radio. The old war buff's sharp as a tack, doesn't miss a beat.

"Power's out everywhere," he stammers. Even that tough old nut is sounding shaken. " Huge crevasses, people heading to the high school. But I don't know how – most of the roads are gone."

"Okay, we're getting our act together," Nicole says. "Getting these guys out, even if they crawl or we have to drag them down. I'll go down and check things out, be back in a minute."

"Good plan," Eddie says, frowning. He's come prepared, his cane snapped to a walker, and a bag of juices, crackers, quilts and blankets on top.

Lewis smells smoke, big-time. Sprinklers not kicking in. He's got a few residents huddled, holding hands. He's trying to use a calm voice. "Keep together, that's right."

Nicole's out of breath from running back up the stairwell. As she opens the door a burning cylinder comes shooting out of the Complex Care unit next door. Like a Cruise missile. The shock drops Nicole to the floor. For a minute she's dazed. And Lewis feels himself reaching out to her in slow motion.

Then an implosion. Shock wave. Blown transformers outside the window sending up fireworks. A rumble from beneath the building, like the sound of thunder gone from the sky to the ground. The building shimmying, giving way.

It's like a roller coaster, going only down. The lounge laid on its side, strangely intact. Or so it seems until the roof crumbles like peanut brittle. Concrete beams, steel studs, the snapping sound of plywood. Two-by-fours flying through the air, sheets of drywall ripped apart like blown bits of paper. A cloud of dust.

Nicole screaming, "Cover your mouths. With anything!"

At the edges of the monster hole, things keep settling and falling into the void below. Clumps of earth. As though outside has become inside, and the inside is gone.

There's mostly a silence now. An eerie whoosh, as if from an ocean breeze. And coughing, someone coughing.

Lewis can feel it, in the darkness. The empty leash. Lucky gone. No silly barking to be heard.

"I can't breathe." A faint voice from the darkness.

Lewis, his own throat dry and rasping, " Eddie, is that you?" Nothing.

Sewer smell. An overwhelming rotten-egg stench. Gas leak.

Lewis suddenly sees a different shade of darkness. What look like stars in the heavens, through the dust fog. Climbing up, at an angle, on his hands and knees.

He finds a wingback chair. Feels his way along, the floor surface changing from carpet to a rubbery texture. Then iron bars, tight together; the outside balcony rails. Iron is good.

But his legs are shaking, and he can't get far without more debris sliding on top of him. Then that whooshing sound of a distant ocean turns into the angry sound of water close at hand, forcing its way through the rubble.

Groundwater, running through the pockets of air in the mangled dark, louder, louder. A gusher.

Lewis hears another chopper, more loudly over what sounds like heavy rain. He pulls himself toward the swirling pinpoints of light. Yells for Lucky. For Eddie. For Nicole.

"I'm over here," Nicole says, in a croaky voice not quite her own. "Kind of stuck in the mud."

One out of three ain't bad, Lewis thinks.

She's not far below him, but it'll be tricky if she dislodges anything, gets herself deeper in the muck. He doesn't know whether to tell her to stay put or climb like blazes.

Her voice is closer now, saying "stay, stay, stay." With an odd whimper attached.

"I've got her," she says. Passing him Lucky in the dark.

Lucky's humble for once, cowering by his side, ears pinned back. But she seems fine when he squeezes her small firm body. It frightens Lewis, that Nicole might have been a-goner, just trying to reach the darn dog.

Out of the darkness, "Yoo-hoo. Is anyone there? Help me—I've been trying to climb out."

"Is that you, Dot?" Nicole asks.

But of course she can't hear a thing. "Yoo-hoo, " she repeats. "I need some help here."

"Hold your horses there, Dot. We'll be coming around the mountain when we come." A wheezing voice, nearly a whisper.

Lewis can't believe it. "That you, Eddie?"

"Yep, and I've got Dot alongside." More wheezing. "Although I sure could use my puffer. Seem to have lost it in the dust-up." He snorts at his own joke.

"You tough old bugger," Lewis says. He's so impressed with the old guy, he wants to razz him a little. "Any chance you can get anything on that radio of yours?"

"I'm trying," Eddie coughs out. "Hold on, hold on. Okay – got something. They're calling it the Cascadia – it runs from Cape Mendocina, in California. We caught the tail end – Seattle's halfway gone. Thousands—"

Eddie's gasping.

"Don't talk," Lewis says.

But Eddie persists, like the old trooper he is. "The mayor's on –" he croaks. "Three sections of town gone, landslides everywhere."

"I think our best bet is to move towards the elevator," Lewis says. He's figured out that's the bit of sky he can see. "Strong part of the building, some air down the shaft maybe. Let's go". He's suddenly taking charge, and liking the feeling.

The five, including Lucky, hunker down, Dorothy propped up against the wall. She's pooped, you can tell.

"Exercise classes coming in handy," she says.

They all laugh, but it's the nervous kind. Where you want to scream instead.

Nicole's the first to notice; she takes the flashlight Eddie's thought to bring along. There's blood pooling in the grit below Dot.

"I think you're hurt, Dot. Let me take a look," Nicole says.

"We finally got lettuce on those turkey sandwiches, didn't we?" Dot replies. She hasn't heard a word they're saying. "I'm grateful for that."

Eddie pulls out a bottle of water from his jacket. Extends the water to Dot.

Dot perks up. "Oh, I have cookies, almost forgot." She pats her pocket; she keeps them there for Lucky.

Something moves across the floor and before anyone can see what it is, Lucky has it in her mouth. One fling, one shake—and Lucky standing guard over it.

Lewis points the flashlight in the dog's direction. But the light's dim, growing dimmer by the minute. They all stare at the dead rat, saying nothing.

"I've lost my appetite," Eddie whispers, with a wince.

Lewis is wondering whether they had rats in the building all along, or whether it's an ominous sign of things to come.

"It was just trying to survive," Dot says.

"Like we were, in the trenches. Lots of rats, I can tell you," Eddie says. He's having flashbacks to the war, and who can blame him.

Lucky's got back her old gusto, shows her teeth at Lewis when he grabs the creature with the cookie bag, turned inside out.

"Lots of practice with a poop bag," he says.

"It's an interesting life I've lived," Dot says, totally out of sync. And with a glint in her eye. "My husband was a genius at business – among other things," she adds, as if she's wrapping things up.

"Me too," Eddie says, "although I should have checked the batteries on the damn flashlight."

Lewis isn't liking where this conversation is heading. "Shhh, listen!" he says. Noises from above, far away voices echo down the shaft.

It's hard to say whether it's someone trapped, or rescuers. Dot hasn't heard a thing, and she's leaning over, sliding down the wall, finally hits the prone position with a thump.

Nicole feels for a pulse; but her watery eyes give it away.

"It's fast and faint," she says. Not a good sign."

Meanwhile Eddie's rasping like a train on a steep incline.

Nicole stares at the shifting darkness. Deeper patches of black, and then shades of something slightly less opaque. "Do you believe, Lewis? You know, in life after death, all that stuff?"

'I don't know anymore. Went to church on Sunday, even studied theology – was a good Catholic boy once. All I know is it's a long time on earth, if it's for nothing."

"How does the spiel go, the so-called Act of Contrition? The thing you say before you die, and then you're covered, you're in …?

"Oh My God, I am heartily sorry for having offended Thee. ...Lewis recites. "I forget the rest. I guess it's purgatory for me," he says. "Sort of like that old girlfriend I had, who said, if you prove to me in six months, quit drinking, work real hard, then maybe...."

"I've been proving it and proving it, raising the two boys by myself, ..." Nicole counters.

Lewis feels like a schmuck for having raised a prickly subject. "You've earned your wings," he says, " ... Ding, ding, ding."

He doesn't need to explain it.

Nicole pipes up – "That's my favourite Christmas movie. Good old Jimmy Stewart ..."

"I played Clarence once ... in a play," Lewis says. "Had to pretend to be wiser than I was."

"I can't sit here doing nothing," Nicole adds after a thoughtful silence. "I'm going back to try and grab what you call my peace-love bag – I had snacks, some first aid stuff."

She lies on her back, puts both legs up against the pile of debris and pushes. Lewis slides a metal bar beneath a heap of splintered two-by-fours. Tries a little leverage. The pile shifts and there's a shudder.

"Jesus, Nicole, get back," Lewis warns. But she's already crawling through a small opening beside a twisted iron railing.

"I'm good," she says, "I can smell fresh air, I swear it."

And then there's a god-awful sound, like a heavy deck of cards, falling. And falling. And a voice that sounds like Nicole's. Screaming, and then sounding foggier and faint. Far away. She's buried, somewhere beyond him.

"Nicole, Nicole? Are you okay? Are you there?"

Lewis grabs a stick of wood and bangs on a steed stud that's staring him in the eye. Bang bang, bang bang.

Eddie says, in a small, peaked voice, "That's not Morris code, not the right message."

Lewis is panicking now, throwing things left and right, a whole wall seems to have collapsed. He's thinking he might have caused it, made it happen.

"Hey take it easy down there," someone says. "How many are you? We're going to get you out!"

The voice gets louder, and there's suddenly an opening, a beam of brightness through the dust. Two men suspended in the shaft, on ropes, wearing high-powered lights on their helmets. It's blinding after they've been in the dark.

"Four and a dog," Lewis says. "One out cold, and

another buried – just now." Lewis is shaking so badly just thinking about Nicole, he's in a cold sweat. "And one guy needs his puffer. Barely holding on," he adds.

"I'm dropping down a bag. A light, inhaler, some water. And masks – put them on, you'll breathe better. Name's Tommy," he says. "We'll be right back …..to get you all out."

The ground starts shaking as Lewis crawls over to Eddie, gives him a little squirt of the one-size-fits-all inhaler they carry in first aid kits. "When we get out, we're going to have steak and eggs, …But bring your puffer, okay?"

He's trying to crack a joke but there's no laughing from Eddie. Just a croak on the out-breath as he tries for air.

It's taking forever to get those guys down here. Lewis crawls back to where he last saw Nicole shimmy through the debris. He shouts for her again, shines his light up against the mountain of rubble. Lucky's sniffing the ground, scratching and clawing. She's pawing at something. Lewis sees a scrap of woven material, a strap – oh my god, it's her hippy bag, with the colourful Mayan design. He sees a frayed bit of red yarn, and follows it …

He moves a few rocks, and then a few more. It's taking everything he's got to keep his arms steady and strong. Everything shifts and settles in a new pattern. He can see her now; she's in a pocket, somewhat protected between a couple of bent iron railings. Her shoulder's crooked, her head at an odd angle. Eyes closed, not saying a thing. Not moving.

He can just reach the back of her head, and holds it firmly on either side. He saw this in a movie, how you keep someone from breaking their neck, making things worse.

She's cool to the touch, doesn't flutter an eye.

Lewis hasn't said a prayer in years. But he's bargaining now, hedging his bets. He says he'll give anything just to have her back.

And like an answer of sorts, Tommy's finally dangling in the shaft. Another guy drops to all fours, crawls toward Nicole.

"Careful, just be careful. Her head, her back – I've been holding her still, " Lewis hisses.

"We got it, we'll keep her steady –" Tommy says. Lewis can hardly bear to watch as they shift the piping and plaster, find the rest of Nicole, one of her pant legs soaked in blood.

They edge her onto a stretcher, and he's barking orders at them to be careful, to not be so rough – he can't help himself. They have to pulley her up at an angle and the whole time she's being lifted, Lewis can't help thinking they'll drop her.

"Hey," Tommy says, "she's a good friend, eh?"

"You betcha. I'd marry her if I could …"

"No worries, we'll take care of her. And stay cool, you're shaking like a leaf. We'll be back in a bit."

Lewis doesn't want to tell the fellow that he always shakes, except today it's worse. He hasn't had his meds, and he made a plea bargain with the guy upstairs.

Of course Lucky thinks the whole shtick of being lifted in a harness is just too exciting; she almost wriggles out of the makeshift carrier to keep her secure. Nicole's woven bag, from her travels in Guatemala, she once told Lewis. Lucky's foolish grin as she yips and yaps, just peeking out the top.

When Lewis makes it to fresh air, the town seems unfamiliar, everything out of place. The roads out of joint, the toppled, half-sunk buildings smoking, and people everywhere, in wrapped blankets or torn clothes, their faces stunned. Disbelieving.

Wait til Orvar hears about this, Lewis thinks. He wants to remind him who got buried, and who the real hero was, all those years ago in the snow. He thinks he knows now how it went, whose fault it was. And this time, if he fesses up, they'll agree on it.

The hospital up the coast – or at least a good part of it—has managed to stay upright, workable. Lewis hesitates. Cautiously peeks his head into the room.

A nurse steps brusquely into his path. "May I help you?"

"I'm just looking for a friend," Lewis says. "Nicole Peters."

"So you're not family?" she asks. The nurse has a guarded look, as testy as Lucky with a bone. "She's resting."

"It's okay, let her sleep," he says. He turns to leave.

"Are you Eddie?" she asks. "She's been saying Lucky and Eddie a lot. And Dot."

No Lewis, he realizes, feeling more than a little hurt. He shuffles past two teenage boys, one who looks a lot like Nicole. Chiseled face, with that little bump on the bridge of his nose. The piercing eyes. Now *there's* family, he thinks.

And then he hears his name, "Lewis! Lewis!" That bullish nurse bellowing after him.

He turns and limps back -- on the heels of those two boys.

He's shocked to see her. She's wearing one of those halo dealies, screwed right into her skull so she can't move her head or neck, even slightly. Must have a cracked vertebra then. And one of her legs is hoisted toward the ceiling.

But she can move her hands, he can see that much. He feels awkward standing there, the boys, one on each side, squeezing her fingers. Her eyes are closed, but she's smiling, faintly.

One of the boys asks, "What's this, mom?" He lets go her hand, and in her palm a small red heart-shaped tag. Lucky. And Lewis' old phone no.

He's been living at a new address. By himself, and doing not too badly.

"Silly dog I know," Nicole says. Now she's looking straight at Lewis. Eyes as blue and unblinking as ever.

He doesn't know what to say. How to even begin.

"I'm living in a Winnebago, Orvar's solution on wheels," Lewis says. "Eddie comes over and we play crib. He tells me Dot's not doing too bad, either. Now that she's gotten over the shock of it all. She's living with a sister she never much liked. But we have to change, don't we?"

Nicole can't nod her head to agree. But she moves

her lips, makes it easy for Lewis. "I heard you, you know. What you said when they were lifting me out. I heard what you said."

And she closes her eyes again, her smile spreading.

Portrait of Lucky Lou by Makiko Kitama

Lucky On a Mission.

Bell Bottoms And Paws

About The Author

"The Red Thread", the first of a series of short stories, by Robert MacDonald. He has previously written and produced three plays. "Home Care …. A Love Story", "The Writer" and "An Irish Breakfast". The journey continues as Robert weaves another story about small town life and the characters who live there. He lives in Gibsons, B.C., and is working on his second second short story.

"Orvar and Lewis"

The Red Thread is dedicated to my father

Made in the USA
Charleston, SC
15 June 2016